The WIDOW and the PARROT

VIRGINIA WOOLF

The WIDOW and the PARROT

Illustrated by Julian Bell *Afterword by* Quentin Bell

HBJ

Harcourt Brace Jovanovich, Publishers
San Diego   New York   London

Requests for permission to make copies of any
part of the work should be mailed to:
Permissions, Harcourt Brace Jovanovich, Publishers,
Orlando, Florida 32887.

Library of Congress Cataloging-in-Publication Data
Woolf, Virginia.
The widow and the parrot.
Summary: When the house she has inherited from her
miserly brother burns down, a widow from Yorkshire
adopts a parrot which leads her to a hidden treasure.
[1. Parrots—Fiction.   2. Buried treasure—Fiction.
3. England—Fiction]   I. Bell, Julian, ill.   II. Title.
PZ7.W88155Wi   1988   [E]   87-19747
ISBN 0-15-296783-4

First edition
A B C D E

The illustrations in this book were done in a variety of ink washes
on Arches paper primed with liquid gesso.
The text type was set in Caslon 540 and
the display type was set in Caslon Openface by
Thompson Type, San Diego, California.
Printed and bound by South China Printing Company,
Quarry Bay, Hong Kong
Production supervision by Eileen McGlone and
Warren Wallerstein
Designed by Nancy J. Ponichtera

The WIDOW and the PARROT

Some fifty years ago Mrs Gage, an elderly widow, was sitting in her cottage in a village called Spilsby in Yorkshire. Although lame, and rather short sighted she was doing her best to mend a pair of clogs, for she had only a few shillings a week to live on. As she hammered at the clog, the postman opened the door and threw a letter into her lap.

It bore the address 'Messrs Stagg and Beetle, 67 High Street, Lewes, Sussex.'

Mrs Gage opened it and read:

'Dear Madam; We have the honour to inform you of the death of your brother Mr Joseph Brand.'

'Lawk a mussy,' said Mrs Gage. 'Old brother Joseph gone at last!'

'He has left you his entire property,' the letter went on, 'which consists of a dwelling house, stable, cucumber frames, mangles, wheelbarrows &c &c in the village of Rodmell, near Lewes. He also bequeaths to you his entire fortune; Viz: £3,000 (three thousand pounds) sterling.'

Mrs Gage almost fell into the fire with joy. She had not seen her brother for many years, and, as he did not even acknowledge the Christmas card which she sent him every year, she thought that his miserly habits, well known to her from childhood, made him grudge even a penny stamp for a reply. But now it had all turned out to her advantage. With three thousand pounds, to say nothing of house &c &c, she could live in great luxury for ever.

She determined that she must visit Rodmell at once. The village clergyman, the Rev Samuel Tallboys, lent her two pound ten, to pay her fare, and by next day all preparations for her journey were complete. The most important of these was the care of her dog Shag during her absence, for in spite of her poverty she was devoted to animals, and often went short herself rather than stint her dog of his bone.

She reached Lewes late on a Tuesday night in November. In those days, I must tell you, there was no bridge over the river at Southease, nor had the road to Newhaven yet been made. To reach Rodmell it was necessary to cross the river Ouse by a ford, traces of which still exist, but this could only be attempted at low tide, when the stones on the river bed appeared above the water. Mr Stacey, the farmer, was going to Rodmell in his cart, and he kindly offered to take Mrs Gage with him. They reached Rodmell about nine o'clock at night and Mr Stacey obligingly pointed out to Mrs Gage the house at the end of the village which had been left her by her brother. Mrs Gage knocked at the door. There was no answer. She knocked again. A very strange high voice shrieked out 'Not at home.' She was so much taken aback that if she had not heard footsteps coming she would have run away. However the door was opened by an old village woman, by name Mrs Ford.

'Who was that shrieking out "Not at home"?' said Mrs Gage.

'Drat the bird!' said Mrs Ford very peevishly, pointing to a large grey parrot. 'He almost screams my head off. There he sits all day humped up on his perch like a monument screeching "Not at home" if ever you go near him.' He was a very handsome bird, as Mrs Gage could see; but his feathers were sadly neglected. 'Perhaps he is unhappy, or he may be hungry,' she said. But Mrs Ford said it was temper merely; he was a seaman's parrot and had learnt his language in the east. However, she added, Mr Joseph was very fond of him, had called him James; and, it was said, talked to him as if he were a rational being. Mrs Ford soon left. Mrs Gage at once went to her box and fetched some sugar which she had with her and offered it to the parrot, saying in a very kind tone that she meant him no harm, but was his old master's sister, come to take possession of the house, and she would

see to it that he was as happy as a bird could be. Taking a lantern she
next went round the house to see what sort of property her brother had
left her. It was a bitter disappointment. There were holes in all the
carpets. The bottoms of the chairs had fallen out. Rats ran along the
mantelpiece. There were large toadstools growing through the kitchen
floor. There was not a stick of furniture worth seven pence halfpenny;
and Mrs Gage only cheered herself by thinking of the three thousand
pounds that lay safe and snug in Lewes Bank.

She determined to set off to Lewes next day in order to claim her money from Messrs Stagg and Beetle the solicitors, and then to return home as quick as she could. Mr Stacey, who was going to market with some fine Berkshire pigs, again offered to take her with him, and as they drove he told her some terrible stories of young people who had been drowned through trying to cross the river at high tide. A great disappointment was in store for the poor old woman directly she got in to Mr Stagg's office.

'Pray take a seat, Madam,' he said, looking very solemn and grunting slightly. 'The fact is,' he went on, 'that you must prepare to face some very disagreeable news. Since I wrote to you I have gone carefully through Mr Brand's papers. I regret to say that I can find no trace whatever of the three thousand pounds. Mr Beetle, my partner, went himself to Rodmell and searched the premises with the utmost care. He found absolutely nothing—no gold, silver, or valuables of any kind—except a fine grey parrot which I advise you to sell for whatever he will fetch. His language, Benjamin Beetle said, is very extreme. But that is neither here nor there. I much fear you have had your journey for nothing. The premises are dilapidated; and of course our expenses are considerable.' Here he stopped, and Mrs Gage well knew that he wished her to go. She was almost crazy with disappointment. Not only had she borrowed two pound ten from the Rev Samuel Tallboys, but she would return home absolutely empty handed, for the parrot James would have to be sold to pay her fare. It was raining hard, but Mr Stagg did not press her to stay, and she was too beside herself with sorrow to care what she did. In spite of the rain she started to walk back to Rodmell across the meadows.

Mrs Gage, as I have already said, was lame in her right leg. At the best of times she walked slowly, and now, what with her disappointment and the mud on the bank her progress was very slow indeed. As she plodded along, the day grew darker and darker, until it was as much as she could do to keep on the raised path by the river side. You might have heard her grumbling as she walked, and complaining of her crafty brother Joseph, who had put her to all this trouble 'Express,' she said, 'to plague me. He was always a cruel little boy when we were children,' she went on. 'He liked worrying the poor insects, and I've

known him trim a hairy caterpillar with a pair of scissors before my very eyes. He was such a miserly varmint too. He used to hide his pocket money in a tree, and if anyone gave him a piece of iced cake for tea, he cut the sugar off and kept it for his supper. I make no doubt he's all aflame at this very moment in Hell fire, but what's the comfort of that to me?' she asked, and indeed it was very little comfort, for she ran slap into a great cow which was coming along the bank, and rolled over and over in the mud.

She picked herself up as best she could and trudged on again. It seemed to her that she had been walking for hours. It was now pitch dark and she could scarcely see her own hand before her nose. Suddenly she bethought her of Farmer Stacey's words about the ford. 'Lawk a mussy,' she said, 'however shall I find my way across? If the tide's in, I shall step into deep water and be swept out to sea in a jiffy! Many's the couple that been drowned here; to say nothing of horses, carts, herds of cattle, and stacks of hay.'

Indeed what with the dark and the mud she had got herself into a pretty pickle. She could hardly see the river itself, let alone tell whether she had reached the ford or not. No lights were visible anywhere, for, as you may be aware, there is no cottage or house on that side of the river nearer than Asheham House, lately the seat of Mr Leonard Woolf. It seemed that there was nothing for it but to sit down and wait for the morning. But at her age, with the rheumatics in her system, she might well die of cold. On the other hand, if she tried to cross the river it was almost certain that she would be drowned. So miserable was her state that she would gladly have changed places with one of the cows in the field. No more wretched old woman could have been found in the whole county of Sussex; standing on the river bank, not knowing whether to sit or to swim, or merely to roll over in

the grass, wet though it was, and sleep or freeze to death, as her fate decided.

At that moment a wonderful thing happened. An enormous light shot up into the sky, like a gigantic torch, lighting up every blade of grass, and showing her the ford not twenty yards away. It was low tide, and the crossing would be an easy matter if only the light did not go out before she had got over.

'It must be a comet or some such wonderful monstrosity,' she said as she hobbled across. She could see the village of Rodmell brilliantly lit up in front of her.

'Bless us and save us!' she cried out. 'There's a house on fire—thanks be to the Lord'—for she reckoned that it would take some minutes at least to burn a house down, and in that time she would be well on her way to the village.

'It's an ill wind that blows nobody any good,' she said as she hobbled along the Roman road. Sure enough, she could see every inch of the way, and was almost in the village street when for the first time it struck her, 'Perhaps it's my own house that's blazing to cinders before my eyes!'

She was perfectly right.

A small boy in his nightgown came capering up to her and cried out, 'Come and see old Joseph Brand's house ablaze!'

All the villagers were standing in a ring round the house handing buckets of water which were filled from the well in Monks House kitchen, and throwing them on the flames. But the fire had got a strong hold, and just as Mrs Gage arrived, the roof fell in.

'Has anybody saved the parrot?' she cried.

'Be thankful you're not inside yourself, Madam,' said the Rev James Hawkesford, the clergyman. 'Do not worry for the dumb creatures. I make no doubt the parrot was mercifully suffocated on his perch.'

But Mrs Gage was determined to see for herself. She had to be held back by the village people, who remarked that she must be crazy to hazard her life for a bird.

'Poor old woman,' said Mrs Ford, 'she has lost all her property, save one old wooden box, with her night things in it. No doubt we should be crazed in her place too.'

So saying, Mrs Ford took Mrs Gage by the hand and led her off to her own cottage, where she was to sleep the night. The fire was now extinguished, and everybody went home to bed.

But poor Mrs Gage could not sleep. She tossed and tumbled thinking of her miserable state, and wondering how she could get back to Yorkshire and pay the Rev Samuel Tallboys the money she owed him. At the same time she was even more grieved to think of the fate of the poor parrot James. She had taken a liking to the bird, and thought that he must have an affectionate heart to mourn so deeply for the death of old Joseph Brand, who had never done a kindness to any human creature. It was a terrible death for an innocent bird, she thought; and if only she had been in time, she would have risked her own life to save his.

She was lying in bed thinking these thoughts when a slight tap at the window made her start. The tap was repeated three times over. Mrs Gage got out of bed as quickly as she could and went to the window. There, to her utmost surprise, sitting on the window ledge was an enormous bird. The rain had stopped and it was a fine moonlight night. She was greatly alarmed at first, but soon recognised the grey parrot, James, and was overcome with joy at his escape. She opened the window, stroked his head several times, and told him to come in. The parrot replied by gently shaking his head from side to side, then flew to the ground, walked away a few steps, looked back as if to see whether Mrs Gage were coming, and then returned to the window sill, where she stood in amazement.

'The creature has more meaning in its acts than we humans know,' she said to herself. 'Very well, James,' she said aloud, talking to him as though he were a human being, 'I'll take your word for it. Only wait a moment while I make myself decent.'

So saying she pinned on a large apron, crept as lightly as possible downstairs, and let herself out without rousing Mrs Ford.

The parrot James was evidently satisfied. He now hopped briskly a few yards ahead of her in the direction of the burnt house. Mrs Gage

followed as fast as she could. The parrot hopped, as if he knew his way perfectly, round to the back of the house, where the kitchen had originally been. Nothing now remained of it except the brick floor, which was still dripping with the water which had been thrown to put out the fire. Mrs Gage stood still in amazement while James hopped about, pecking here and there, as if he were testing the bricks with his beak. It was a very uncanny sight, and had not Mrs Gage been in the habit of living with animals, she would have lost her head, very likely, and hobbled back home. But stranger things yet were to happen. All this time the parrot had not said a word. He suddenly got into a state

of the greatest excitement, fluttering his wings, tapping the floor re-
peatedly with his beak, and crying so shrilly, 'Not at home! Not at
home!' that Mrs Gage feared that the whole village would be roused.

'Don't take on so James; you'll hurt yourself,' she said soothingly.
But he repeated his attack on the bricks more violently than ever.

'Whatever can be the meaning of it?' said Mrs Gage, looking carefully at the kitchen floor. The moonlight was bright enough to show
her a slight unevenness in the laying of the bricks, as if they had been
taken up and then relaid not quite flat with the others. She had fas-
tened her apron with a large safety pin, and she now prised this pin

between the bricks and found that they were only loosely laid together. Very soon she had taken one up in her hands. No sooner had she done this than the parrot hopped onto the brick next to it, and, tapping it smartly with his beak, cried, 'Not at home!' which Mrs Gage understood to mean that she was to move it. So they went on taking up the bricks in the moonlight until they had laid bare a space some six feet by four and a half. This the parrot seemed to think was enough. But what was to be done next?

Mrs Gage now rested, and determined to be guided entirely by the behaviour of the parrot James. She was not allowed to rest for long.

After scratching about in the sandy foundations for a few minutes, as you may have seen a hen scratch in the sand with her claws, he unearthed what at first looked like a round lump of yellowish stone. His excitement became so intense that Mrs Gage now went to his help. To her amazement she found that the whole space which they had uncovered was packed with long rolls of these round yellow stones, so neatly laid together that it was quite a job to move them. But what could they be? And for what purpose had they been hidden here? It was not until they had removed the entire layer on the top, and next a piece of oil cloth which lay beneath them, that a most miraculous sight was displayed before their eyes—there, in row after row, beautifully polished, and shining brightly in the moonlight, were thousands of brand new sovereigns!!!

This, then, was the miser's hiding place; and he had made sure that no one would detect it by taking two extraordinary precautions. In the first place, he had built a kitchen range over the spot where his treasure lay hid, so that unless the fire had destroyed it, no one could have guessed its existence; and secondly he had coated the top layer of sovereigns with some sticky substance, then rolled them in the earth, so that if by chance one had been laid bare no one would have suspected that it was anything but a pebble such as you may see for yourself any day in the garden. Thus, it was only by the extraordinary coincidence of the fire and the parrot's sagacity that old Joseph's craft was defeated.

Mrs Gage and the parrot now worked hard and removed the whole hoard—which numbered three thousand pieces, neither more nor less—placing them in her apron which was spread upon the ground. As the three thousandth coin was placed on the top of the pile, the parrot flew up into the air in triumph and alighted very gently on the

top of Mrs Gage's head. It was in this fashion that they returned to Mrs Ford's cottage, at a very slow pace, for Mrs Gage was lame, as I have said, and now she was almost weighted to the ground by the contents of her apron. But she reached her room without any one knowing of her visit to the ruined house.

Next day she returned to Yorkshire. Mr Stacey once more drove her into Lewes and was rather surprised to find how heavy Mrs Gage's wooden box had become. But he was a quiet sort of man, and merely

concluded that the kind people at Rodmell had given her a few odds and ends to console her for the dreadful loss of all her property in the fire. Out of sheer goodness of heart Mr Stacey offered to buy the parrot off her for half a crown; but Mrs Gage refused his offer with such indignation, saying that she would not sell the bird for all the wealth of the Indies, that he concluded that the old woman had been crazed by her troubles.

It now only remains to be said that Mrs Gage got back to Spilsby in

safety; took her black box to the Bank; and lived with James the parrot and her dog Shag in great comfort and happiness to a very great age.

It was not till she lay on her death bed that she told the clergyman (the son of the Rev Samuel Tallboys) the whole story, adding that she was quite sure that the house had been burnt on purpose by the parrot James, who, being aware of her danger on the river bank, flew into the scullery, and upset the oil stove which was keeping some scraps warm for her dinner. By this act, he not only saved her from drowning, but brought to light the three thousand pounds, which could have been found in no other manner. Such, she said, is the reward of kindness to animals.

The clergyman thought that she was wandering in her mind. But it is certain that the very moment the breath was out of her body, James the parrot shrieked out, 'Not at home! Not at home!' and fell off his perch stone dead. The dog Shag had died some years previously.

Visitors to Rodmell may still see the ruins of the house, which was burnt down fifty years ago, and it is commonly said that if you visit it in the moonlight you may hear a parrot tapping with his beak upon the brick floor, while others have seen an old woman sitting there in a white apron.

The End

Afterword

Here is an addition, tiny but not uninteresting, to the great corpus of Virginia Woolf's writings. Under what heading shall we place it? Is it fiction? Undoubtedly; but like so much fiction it is also journalism. It was written for a newspaper and commissioned by an editor. I know—I was the editor. I was only 12 or 13 at the time.

My brother and I produced a family newspaper; it was a daily. I made all the illustrations and most of the other matter. From time to time my brother got bored and stopped work. I carried on reporting and inventing the news as best I could until he, exasperated by my spelling, my handwriting, my grammar &c, would take over again. Thus it happened that I asked for a contribution from my aunt Virginia. I knew she was an author, and although I didn't think much of her work—that is to say I had failed to finish *Kew Gardens*—it seemed stupid to have a real author so close at hand and not have her contribute.

The result—'The Widow and the Parrot'—was a tease. We had hoped vaguely for something as funny, as subversive, and as frivolous as Virginia's conversation. Knowing this, she sent us an 'improving story' with a moral, based on the very worst Victorian examples.

The editor was shocked: this was even worse than *Kew Gardens*. He was joined by his senior colleague. Should they publish? After a long and solemn conclave it was decided that it would be unkind to reject the story.

Si jeunesse savait . . .

Quentin Bell

DATE DUE

MAR 27 197			
GAYLORD			PRINTED IN U.S.A.